For my ever wakeful family. —C. M.

For Granmary. —S. H.

Text copyright © 2020 by Colin Meloy.
Illustrations copyright © 2020 by Shawn Harris.

Library of Congress Cataloging-in-Publication Data available.

ISBN 978-1-4521-7805-9

Manufactured in China.

Design by Jennifer Tolo Pierce.
Typeset in Agenda.
The illustrations in this book were printed in three spot-colors.
Original grayscale plates were rendered with India ink, charcoal,
and pencil.

10 9 8 7 6 5 4 3 2 1

Chronicle Books LLC
680 Second Street
San Francisco, California 94107

Chronicle Books—we see things differently.
Become part of our community at
www.chroniclekids.com.

EVERYONE'S AWAKE

WRITTEN BY
COLIN MELOY

ILLUSTRATED BY
SHAWN HARRIS

chronicle books · san francisco

The crickets are all peeping.
The moon shines on the lake.
We should be soundly sleeping.

But everyone's awake.

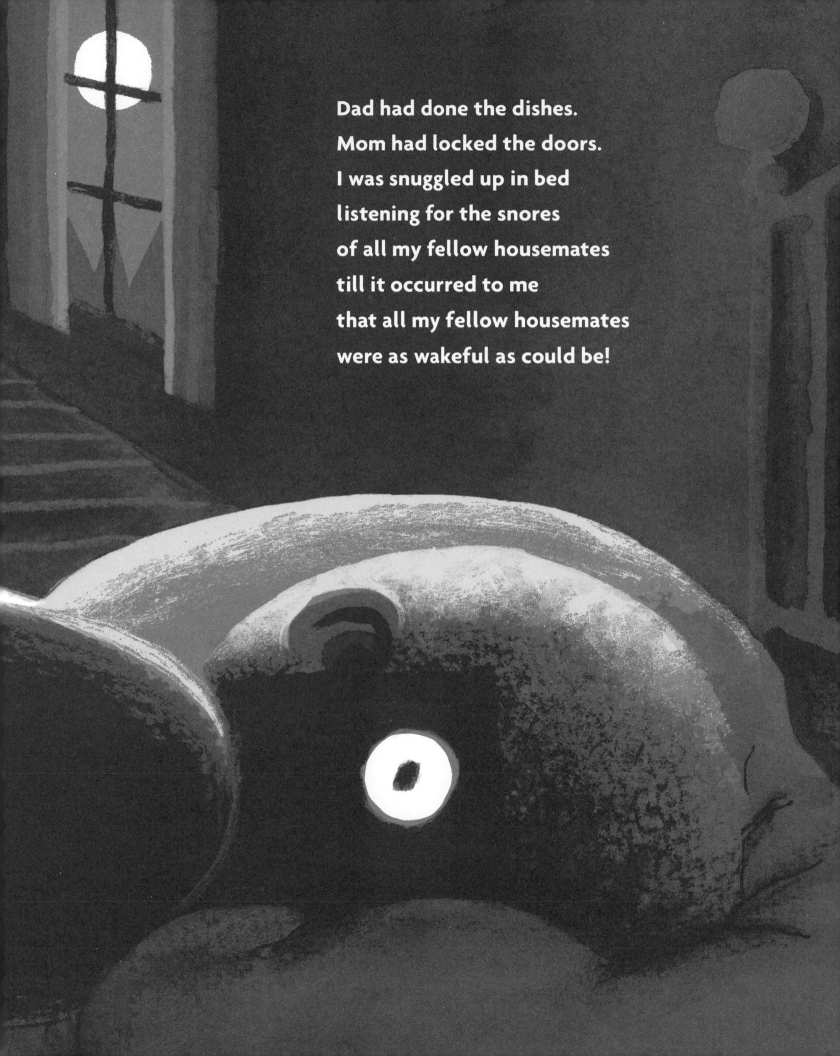

Dad had done the dishes.
Mom had locked the doors.
I was snuggled up in bed
listening for the snores
of all my fellow housemates
till it occurred to me
that all my fellow housemates
were as wakeful as could be!

Grandma's at her needlework.

Dad is baking bread.

**My brother's making laundry lists
of every book he's read.**

**Sister's flossing braces
and reciting Baudelaire**

**while she's locked inside the bathroom
tying plaits into her hair.**

We all got
tucked in early.
A full tomorrow waits.

But here

it's almost midnight.

And everyone's awake!

The cat
is running circles
while the mice
are playing cards.

There's some
unholy racket
being made
out in the yard.

The dog's into the eggnog;

Mom's tap dancing to Prince

while Dad is on the laptop

buying ten-yard bolts of chintz.

My brother's now reciting
every line from Condorman

while my sister is trapezing
from the kitchen ceiling fan.

Dad just rolled the motorbike into the living room
and is practicing Sinatra with the handle of the broom.

I cannot think
what happened
to make us
act this way.
We all were
feeling drowsy
at the dimming
of the day.

But now
nobody's sleeping!
Everyone's awake!
How ever will
we function
in the morning,
for Pete's sake?

Mom is on the rooftop
fixing broken slates.

And Brother's
in the kitchen
juggling
the plates.

Sister's donned a headband and is prepping for a run.

While not asleep, we all at least are getting some things done!

Grandma's on to playing whist
with long-dead
Grandpa Paul,
and the dog
has started throwing darts
against my
bedroom wall.

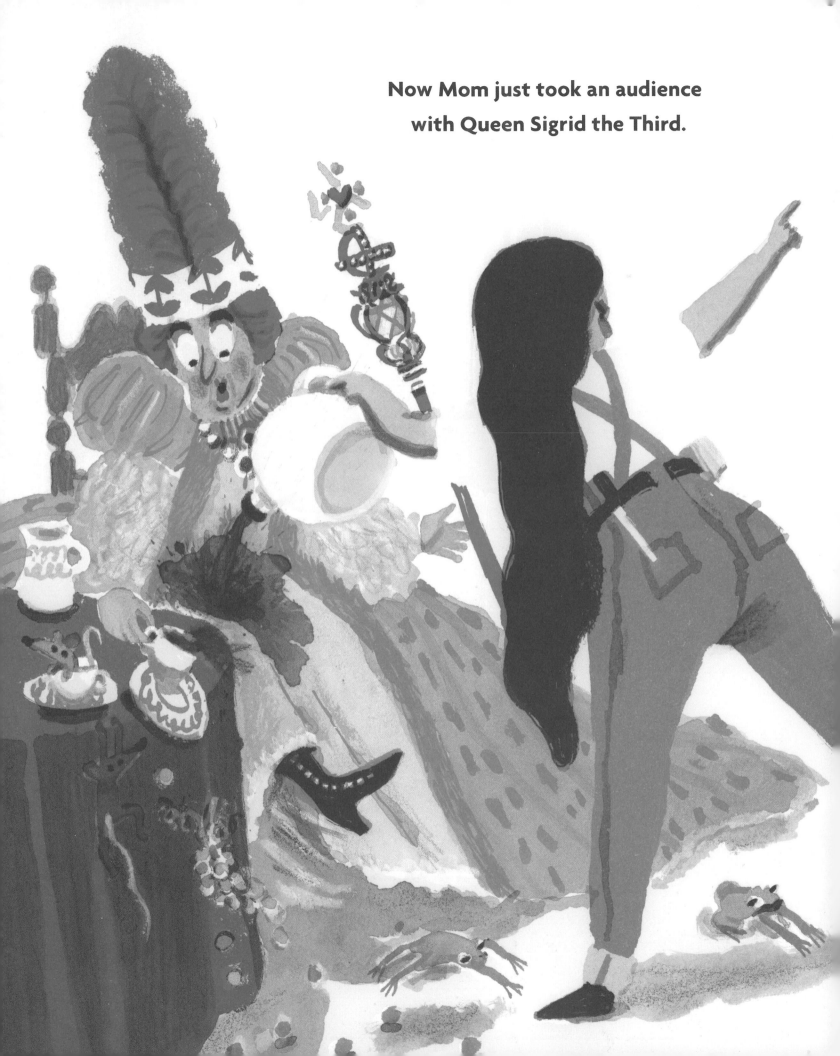

Now Mom just took an audience
with Queen Sigrid the Third.

My brother has just taught the cat a dozen dirty words.

Will we ever settle? Will we ever sleep?
Or will we be reduced into a shambling sleepless heap?

I'm really not quite certain how much more that I can take.
I think that we may just become

FOREVER
EVERYONE
AWAKE

But look:

Sister's on a quiz show.

Dad is
digging
jazz.

Grandma's singing
"Clementine"
with unabashed
pizzazz.

My brother's built a temple from discarded toothpaste tops

while the cat is giving poke tattoos and prank-calling the cops.

My mom just won a Pulitzer;

Dad's sailed
off to war.

Grandma's joined
a miming troupe—

who even
knows what for?

My brother's staged a *coup d'état*
and overthrown the state

while my
sister's joined
the *résistance*

(they never
got on great).

MOM HAS FORCED A TREATY

DAD JUST ANNEXED FRANCE

GRANDMA'S BUILT A GOODYEAR BLIMP FROM DAD'S OLD UNDERPANTS →

And me?
Well, I'm just lying
here awake inside my bed
thinking I should just get up and write a book instead.

Hey, what's all this?
What's happened now?
What light through
window breaks?

The morning's come!
The night is through!
Let's hear no bellyaches!

But just as I walk from my room
and down the staircase creep,
I find the sun is shining down

on everyone,